Delicious English
CARAMEL TREE

www.carameltree.com

No More Mr. Dawdle

CARAMEL TREE

Chapter 1

Mr. Dawdle

Simon's mother called him 'Mr. Dawdle.' Simon was always dawdling around. He dawdled and dawdled. So he was always late. He was late for dinner. He was late for going out. He was late for everything. That was because he always wasted time when he should be getting ready.

Every day, Simon's parents went to
work early in the morning. They asked their
neighbor, Mrs. Crump, to watch Simon.

Mrs. Crump was kind, but she made
Simon eat oatmeal for breakfast. She said it
was good for him. Simon hated oatmeal.

One day, Simon decided to tell his parents that he didn't need Mrs. Crump to come and watch him.

"I am eleven years old," Simon said. "I can get ready by myself."

"We will try it," Mother finally agreed. "But, if you miss the bus, we will have to ask Mrs. Crump to come over in the mornings."

"Thank you!" Simon shouted. He was very proud that his parents trusted him. Mother made Simon write a list. The list would help him not forget anything important before school. The list said:

IMPORTANT THINGS TO DO BEFORE SCHOOL

1. Wash face, comb hair, brush teeth
2. Get dressed - wear clean clothes
3. Open curtains and tidy bed, turn off bedroom light
4. Take library book, homework, and soccer clothes
5. Eat breakfast. No dirty dishes left in the sink!
6. Take lunch
7. Feed Kitty
8. Turn off the TV
9. Lock the door
10. Don't forget the key

Chapter 2
Dawdling

On the first day of school, Simon woke up at 7:30 when his parents left for work.

"No dawdling!" he told Kitty. "The bus comes at 8:00!"

Simon jumped out of bed.

Number 1 on the list was easy. Simon skipped to the bathroom. He washed his face, combed his hair, and brushed his teeth.

Simon hurried back to his room.

The clock read 7:35.

He quickly got dressed. He put on clean clothes, socks, and shoes.

He tied his laces.

No! The laces looked wrong.

He untied them and tied them again. He repeated it three more times until he was happy.

'*Not bad*,' he thought. Besides, his baggy pants covered most of his shoes anyway.

Simon practiced walking with his pants pulled up to make them shorter and show his shoes.

The clock read 7:41.

No more dawdling! He had to do everything on the list before the bus came.

He opened the curtains. That was easy,
too. But that was only part of Number 3. He
quickly straightened his bed. He stood back
and felt proud he remembered to tidy his
bed.

Chapter 3
More Dawdling

Simon jumped down two stairs.

"No more," he sang.

Then, he hopped back up one stair.

"Mrs. Crump!" he shouted.

He jumped down two steps.

"No more," he sang.

Then, he hopped back up one stair.

"Oatmeal!" he screamed.

He hopped down two steps.

"No more Mr. Dawdle!" he yelled.

Then, he spread his arms and jumped

the rest of the way down.

Kitty raced him to the kitchen. Simon
turned on the TV. That reminded him of
Number 8 – Turn off the TV. He turned it off
again.

"Meow," said Kitty.

"Don't worry," said Simon. "Feeding Kitty is Number 7."

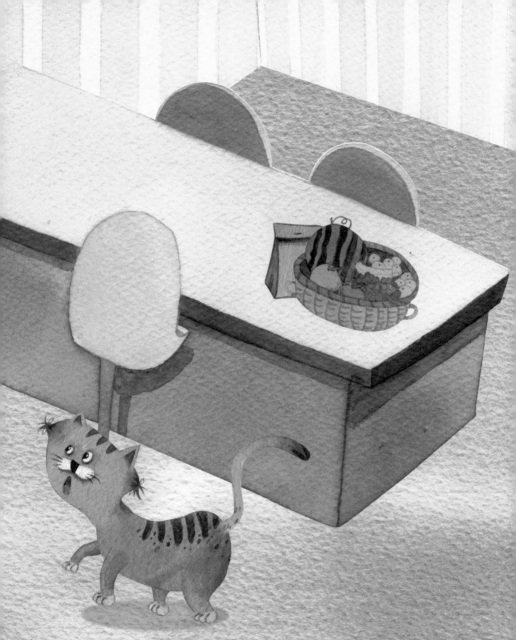

He looked at the list. "I should put 'Don't forget the key' before 'Lock the door,'" he told Kitty.

07:45
brush teeth
dressed-wear clean clothes
en curtains and tidy bed, turn off bedroom light
ake library book, homework, and soccer clothes
t breakfast. No dirty dishes left in the sink!
ke lunch
eed kitty
Turn off the TV
ock the door
Don't forget the key

Simon looked in a drawer for a pencil. He found his old click pencil. He clicked the pencil once. Then he clicked it twice. Then two more times. The pencil was too long now! He carefully pushed it back in. After trying three more times, he finally decided it was just right to write with.

The clock read 7:45.

No more dawdling!

Chapter 4
Even More Dawdling!

Simon poured his favorite cereal into a bowl. *'No More Oatmeal,'* he smiled.

First, he poured too much, so he put some back into the box. Then he put too much back, so he poured some more!

Number 5 was more complicated than it
needed to be.

When he thought he had just the right
amount, he turned to get the milk from the
fridge.

That's when he saw the brown bag on
the counter.

'*Great!*' Number 6 was next – Take lunch.
Simon stuffed the brown bag into his
backpack.

"Meow," said Kitty.

"I know!" said Simon. "Feeding Kitty is Number 7. Let me eat first or this stuff gets soggy."

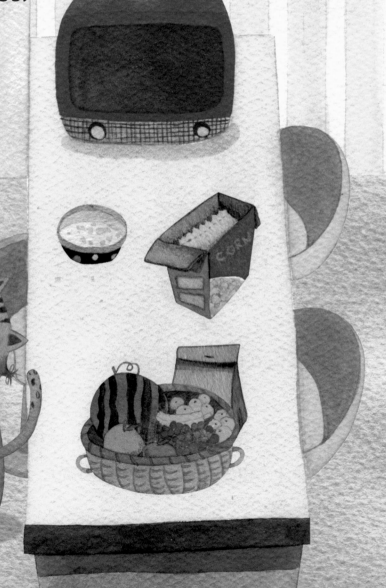

IMPORTANT THINGS TO DO BEFORE SCHOOL
1. Wash face, comb hair, brush teeth
2. Get dressed - wear clean clothes
3. Open curtains and tidy bed. Turn off bedroom light
4. Take library book, homework, and soccer clothes
5. Eat breakfast. No dirty dishes left in the sink!
6. Take lunch
7. Feed Kitty
8. Turn off the TV
9. Lock the door
10. Don't forget the key

"Yowl!" said Kitty.

Maybe Kitty wasn't asking for food.

Simon looked at the list.

"I almost forgot Number 4! Thanks, Kitty," he said. He hopped up the stairs to get his library book, his homework, and soccer clothes.

The library book was on his bedside table. His homework was on his desk. Then he had to find his soccer clothes. It took him a minute to decide which shorts to take. Finally, he packed them all into his backpack.

"Meow!" Kitty jumped onto the bed.

Simon tickled her tummy.

The clock read 7:53.

No more dawdling!

Then, he smelled a strange smell. He peeked into the laundry room. The smell was stronger. *Something was burning!*

Simon saw the iron on the ironing board. The red button was glowing. His mother

Simon looked down. That was three things he did wrong. Perhaps Mrs. Crump would be back tomorrow.

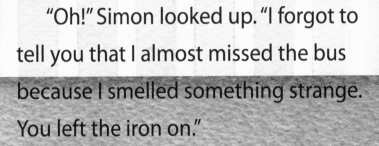

"Oh!" Simon looked up. "I forgot to tell you that I almost missed the bus because I smelled something strange. You left the iron on."

"Oh, no! Good thing I can depend on you!" said Mother.

"I guess we don't need to call Mrs. Crump anymore," Father said proudly.

"As long as he remembers to take the right brown bag!" Mother smiled.

Simon smiled.

No more Mrs. Crump! No more oatmeal! And, no more Mr. Dawdle!

Simon didn't want to eat cat food for lunch again tomorrow.

had forgotten to turn it off!

Simon unplugged the iron and put it away carefully.

Then he hopped down the stairs again.

"You remembered to take your lunch, didn't you?" asked Mother.

"I put the brown bag in my backpack so I wouldn't forget it," he said.

"Meow," said Kitty.

"Did you find the cat food I left in the bag on the counter?" asked Mother.

Simon turned red. "I found it," he mumbled.

"Well, you forgot to turn off the light in your room," Mother said. "And you left your dirty dish in the sink."